# Snow Clothes

Written by Margo Gates

Illustrated by Lisa Hunt

**GRL Consultants, Diane Craig and Monica Marx, Certified Literacy Specialists**

Lerner Publications ◆ Minneapolis

**Note from a GRL Consultant**

This Pull Ahead leveled book has been carefully designed for beginning readers. A team of guided reading literacy experts has reviewed and leveled the book to ensure readers pull ahead and experience success.

Lerner Publications Company
A division of Lerner Publishing Group, Inc.
241 First Avenue North
Minneapolis, MN 55401 USA

For reading levels and more information, look up this title at www.lernerbooks.com.

Main body text set in Mikado 24/41
Typeface provided by Hannes von Doehren.

The images in this book are used with the permission of: Lisa Hunt

**Library of Congress Cataloging-in-Publication Data**

Names: Gates, Margo, author. | Hunt, Lisa (Lisa Jane), 1973– illustrator.
Title: Snow clothes / by Margo Gates ; illustrated by Lisa Hunt.
Description: Minneapolis : Lerner Publications, [2020] | Series: Seasons all around me
    (Pull ahead readers - Fiction) | Includes index.
Identifiers: LCCN 2018056964 (print) | LCCN 2018057808 (ebook) | ISBN 9781541562417
    (eb pdf) | ISBN 9781541558755 (lb : alk. paper) | ISBN 9781541573420 (pb : alk. paper)
Subjects: LCSH: Readers (Primary) | Clothing and dress—Juvenile fiction.
Classification: LCC PE1119 (ebook) | LCC PE1119 .G3847 2020 (print) | DDC 428.6/2—dc23

LC record available at https://lccn.loc.gov/2018056964

Manufactured in the United States of America
2-49335-46256-4/5/2021

# Contents

# Snow Clothes

Mom gives me a coat.

I put on the coat.

Dad gives me a hat.
I put on the hat.

Mom gives me a scarf.

I put on the scarf.

Dad gives me mittens.

I put on the mittens.

Mom gives me boots.
I put on the boots.

# I am ready to play.

# Did You See It?

boots

coat

hat

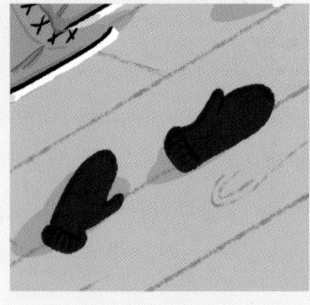
mittens

scarf

snow

# Index

## After Reading

Ask students questions about the book and the book's topic:

1. What clothes does the girl put on to go out in the snow?
2. Does the setting of this story change? Find that part in the story.
3. Does the book remind you of something you have done?

## Word Study

**High-Frequency Word Practice**
Teacher directions: Give each student a whiteboard and dry-erase marker. Have students practice writing the words "gives," "me," and "put." Have students say each word as they write it.

**Blending**
Teacher directions: Use the following words to model how to blend words. Say each sound segment in a word and ask students to say the blended word.

boot: /b/ /oo/ /t/
coat: /c/ /oa/ /t/
hat: /h/ /a/ /t/

Example: coat
Teacher says: /c/ /oa/ /t/
What word do you hear?

LEVEL B
AR LEVEL 0.6
AR POINTS 0.5
LEXILE N/A

# Seasons All Around Me

What is it like outside in winter?
What about in spring, summer, and fall?
These are the four seasons. Which is your favorite?

## Fiction Titles in This Series

## Nonfiction Titles in This Series

Fall Leaves

We Like the Summer

Spring Flowers

Winter Fun

ISBN 978-1-5415-7342-0

90000

9 781541 573420

www.lernerbooks.com
GRL: B